I Wonder

I Wonder

Tana Hoban

Green Light Readers
Harcourt Brace & Company
San Diego   New York   London

First Green Light Readers edition 1999
Green Light Readers is a trademark of Harcourt Brace & Company.

Library of Congress Cataloging-in-Publication Data
Hoban, Tana.
I wonder/Tana Hoban.
p. cm.—(Green Light Readers)
Summary: While walking through the park, a child sees a wondrous
variety of animals.
ISBN 0-15-202355-0
ISBN 0-15-202277-5 pb
[1. Animals—Fiction.] I. Title. II. Series.
PZ7.H638Iae 1999
[E]—dc21   98-55237

A C E F D B

As I walk through the soft, green grass,
I wonder about all the animals I see.

A caterpillar bumps and inches along. Where did he come from? Where is he going?

A cobweb sparkles in the morning sun.
Who spun it? Is it hard to spin a web?

Little bugs zip back and forth. Are they happy or sad? Will they be glad when they get home?

A robin is sitting up on a branch. Is he getting set to fly away? Flying must be fun!

Who is that *buzz-buzzing* from blossom to blossom? Something must smell sweet.

There's a zigzag track in the mud. Is this who came along with a wiggle and a jiggle to make it?

A plump frog is sitting at the pond. Will he jump in for a bath? I think he will.

A duck paddles along with ducklings. Are they all quacking at *me* as they swim by?

A kitten is playing in the grass. Is he out for a walk, just like me? I wish I could ask him.

As I walk back home, I wonder…Do all
the animals wonder about me?

What things do *you* see and wonder about?
Use these pages to make a list

1. _____

_____

_____

_____

2. _____

_____

_____

_____

3. _____

_____

_____

_____

4. _____

_____

_____

_____

5. _____

_____

_____

_____

6. _____

_____

_____

_____

7. _____

_____

_____

_____

8. _____

_____

_____

_____

Display type set in Heatwave
Text set in Minion
Color separations by Bright Arts Ltd., Hong Kong
Printed by South China Printing Company, Ltd., Hong Kong
This book was printed on 140-gsm matte art paper.
Production supervision by Stanley Redfern and Ginger Boyer
Designed by Barry Age